A Perfect Name

CHARLENE COSTANZO PICTURES BY LeUyen PHAM

 Dial Books for Young Readers New York

A Note to Parents

In this story Mama and Papa Potamus consider many names for their beloved Little One. Children hearing the tale are likely to ask: "What does my name mean?" There is power in the way we answer. We must do so with care.

It's fun and easy to look up meanings in name books or on websites about the naming process. However, that information alone may limit a child. Every child needs to know that he or she, like Little One, is loved and has many wondrous qualities and abilities. You may wish to incorporate this message and your own naming story into your answer.

Our thoughtful answers will help our children understand that, like Little One, each of us is a gift. In knowing this, may every child find real meaning.

Published by Dial Books for Young Readers
A division of Penguin Putnam Inc.
345 Hudson Street
New York, New York 10014
Text copyright © 2002 by Charlene Costanzo
Pictures copyright © 2002 by LeUyen Pham
All rights reserved
Designed by Kimi Weart
Text set in Breughel
Printed in Hong Kong on acid-free paper

1 3 5 7 9 10 8 6 4 2

Library of Congress Cataloging-in-Publication Data
Costanzo, Charlene.
A perfect name / by Charlene Costanzo ; pictures by LeUyen Pham.
p. cm.
Summary: Mama and Papa Potamus try out
many different names for their newborn daughter before finding
just the right one in time for her naming ceremony.
ISBN 0-8037-2614-7
[1. Names, Personal–Fiction. 2. Hippopotamus–Fiction.]
I. Pham, LeUyen, ill. II. Title.
PZ7.C822 Pe 2002
[E]–dc21   00-063873

The illustrations for this book were prepared with watercolors on Arches cold-pressed paper.

For Anna Victoria and Stephen Albert,
who named me Charlene Ann . . .
and encouraged me to find the meaning of who I am.
In loving memory.
—C.C.

To all those people I met and traveled
with while on safari in South Africa,
November 1999, with fondest memories.
—L.P.

Mama and Papa Potamus sat side by side.

They searched through *The Name Book* one more time.

"Florella?" Mama said.

"Hmm . . . that has a nice sound. What does it mean?" asked Papa.

"Like a flower," said Mama.

Papa rocked the cradle and smiled at sleeping Little One.

"She *is* a pretty flower," he said. "Prettier than all the flowers that grow along the Wada Wada River.

Let's add Florella to the maybe list."

Mama unrolled the maybe list and wrote "Florella" on the bottom,
after names that meant moonbeam, dancing princess, and brave as a bear.
"We can't add any more names to think about, Papa," said Mama.
"We each need to choose one. The naming ceremony is tomorrow."
"I know, Mama," said Papa. "But we must give our daughter
a suitable name—a *perfect* name."

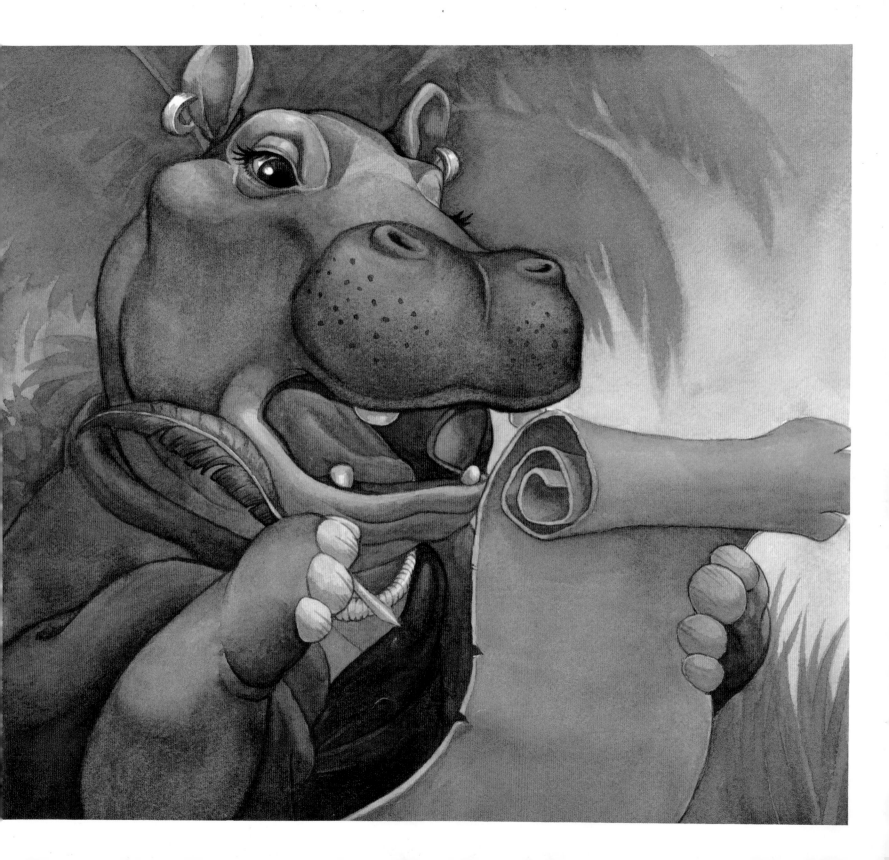

Papa stood up and paced while Mama read out loud.

  Stella

   Lenora

    Mituna

     Philomena

    Fayina

    Golda

    Ethel

     Josephina

"Wait, Mama," he said. "I've got an idea."

Papa whispered softly into Little One's ear.

Mama watched for a smile or a frown.

   Jobina

      Bertha

         Matilda

         Freda

         Luba

         Leah

            Mildred

         Zia

Little One stretched and yawned, but gave them no clue.

Later they watched as she ate and played.
"She's so healthy and wonderful," said Papa.
"Her name should mean that."
"That's Drusilla Merilla," said Mama.

"But look! She's graceful. And talented too."
"Then we should call her Zuza Pandora,"
said Mama.

"And so kind, so friendly."

"Adie Amissa," said Mama.

"But sometimes quiet and shy."

"Myra Modesta," said Mama.

 Papa sighed. "So many beautiful names."

Daylight dimmed.

Again Papa rocked the cradle and studied sleeping Little One.

"What name will fit her?" he asked.

"What name will bring her luck?"

A night creature howled.

"It's late," said Mama.

"Maybe our dreams will help us."

That night Papa dreamed of gifts from the heavens:

warm rain,

cool mud,

sweet grasses,

and his own Little One.

While he slumbered, he snored.
Mama couldn't sleep,
so Mama didn't dream.

Papa woke when a morning bird chattered.
He remembered happy dreams
but still had no name for Little One.
"We'll look for a sign, dear Papa," said Mama.

Distant drums called them to the naming ceremony.
Mama, Papa, and Little One
followed the path to the Wada Wada River,
over the top of the grassy hill,
through the trees,
through the reeds.
Everyone was there,
waiting along the riverbank.

Little One was the first to reach the water.
After a few timid steps she splashed and laughed.
Dipping up and down, she turned ripples into waves.
Thousands of water stars sparkled around her.

"Look at our jewel!" said Mama.
"So heavenly!" said Papa.

Everyone joined Little One.

They made music and shared food.

All day long they danced and sang and celebrated.

When the red sun faced the round yellow moon,
the crowd hushed.
It was time to announce Little One's name.

Mama and Papa Potamus stood before their daughter.
Together they said the ancient prayer wish.
May you grow to be old.
May your dreams come true.
We love you, Little One,
And now we name you . . .

"Dorena," said Papa, "a gift from the heavens."
"Cordula," said Mama, "a jewel in the water."
As Dorena Cordula smiled,
everyone cheered
and said it was a perfect name.